RAIN, RAIN

by Marilyn Greco

illustrated by
Michael Grejniec

**Macmillan
McGraw-Hill**

New York   Farmington

Rain, rain,
Falling down!

Falls in the country,

Falls in town!

Falls on the tigers,
Falls on the clowns.

Falls on our sneakers,
Falls on our crowns.

Falls on the smiles,
Falls on the frowns.

Falls on us right-side-up,
Or when we're upside down!